LETTERS HOME
from
BRAZIL

Marcia S. Gresko

BLACKBIRCH PRESS, INC.

WOODBRIDGE, CONNECTICUT

Published by Blackbirch Press, Inc.
260 Amity Road
Woodbridge, CT 06525

©1999 by Blackbirch Press, Inc.
First Edition

e-mail: staff@blackbirch.com
Web site: www.blackbirch.com

Printed in Singapore

10 9 8 7 6 5 4 3 2 1

Photo Credits
Cover and title page: ©Corel Corporation; pages 4, 6, 7: ©Augusto C.B. Areal; pages 8-31: ©Corel Corporation.

Library of Congress Cataloging-in-Publication Data
Gresko, Marcia S.
Brazil / by Marcia S. Gresko.
   p.   cm. — (Letters home from . . .)
Includes bibliographical references and index.
Summary: Describes some of the sights and experiences on a trip through Brazil, including visits to the capital Brasilia, Ouro Preto, Rio de Janeiro, and the Amazon River.
ISBN 1-56711-407-5
1. Brazil—Juvenile literature. [1. Brazil—Description and travel.] I. Title. II. Series.
F2508.5.G74   1999   99-23480
981—dc21   CIP
                                                                              AC

TABLE OF CONTENTS

Arrival in . . .

Brasília

Today we landed in Brasília, the capital of Brazil. It's winter in North America, but here it's summer time! That's because most of Brazil is located south of the equator, so its seasons are the opposite of those in the Northern Hemisphere. But even during the winter, there's no need for ski jackets or snow boots. Brazil hardly ever gets very cold.

According to the guidebook, Brazil is the fifth-largest country in the world. It covers almost half of the continent of South America. Brazil has tropical jungles and ultra-modern cities, enormous swamplands and dry wastelands, wild frontiers, vast farmlands, and miles of beautiful beaches.

I think Brazil sounds "que legal" (awesome)!

VENEZUELA
GUYANA
SURI-NAME
FR. GUYANA
Atlantic Ocean
COLUMBIA
Belém
Manaus
THE AMAZON RIVER
THE AMAZON
BRAZIL
PERU
Salvador
Ouro Preto
Brasília
I'm here!
BOLIVIA
PARAGUAY
Rio de Janeiro
São Paulo
Atlantic Ocean
Santa Catarina
N
W
E
S
ARGENTINA

Brasília

As we flew over Brasília yesterday, our pilot told us to look out the windows for a surprise—the city's unusual shape. Some passengers thought it looked like a bird in flight, a cross, or a bow and arrow. I agreed with the pilot—from the air Brasília looks like an airplane!

We found out more about Brasília's unique shape during today's city tour. From the deck at the top of the soaring TV Tower, our guide pointed out the city's carefully planned design and its spectacular landmarks. At the "nose" of the airplane is the Palace of the Dawn, the president's home. Important government buildings and cultural attractions are located in the "cabin." The airplane's "wings" contain high-rise apartments, shops, theaters, playgrounds, and schools.

TV Tower

Modern architecture

Fountains in park

Brasília is one of the newest capital cities in the world. Its futuristic look comes from its sleek, modern buildings. The capital was built in the center of the country, far from the crowded coastal cities where three-quarters of Brazilians live. Brasília's central location was chosen to encourage people to settle in Brazil's inland areas.

One of the most unusual buildings is the National Cathedral. It is shaped like a crown. Statues of angels hang from the ceiling and look like they are flying. The ultra-modern Senate and Chamber of Deputies buildings look like two halves of a grapefruit!

Brasília

It's hot in Brasília! (And there aren't too many shady trees here.)

Today we escaped the heat and traffic by visiting one of the city's large shopping centers. The faces in the crowds reminded us that Brazil is a melting pot of different races and cultures. More than half of Brazilians are of white European ancestry. Most others are of mixed racial ancestry. Smaller numbers are of African and native descent.

Brasília's large middle class can afford to shop in attractive stores and eat in good restaurants.

But sadly, many poor people crowd together in favelas, or slums. Their homes are made of scraps of lumber with tin roofs. Few people here have electricity or running water. Life is difficult, especially for children.

Wild pineapple plant

Brasília—Food and Agriculture

Brasília is a great place to eat! It's in Goiás state, which has ranches and farms.
Breakfast usually includes fruit, bread, maybe cheese or meat, and coffee. Even kids drink coffee in Brazil!

A huge lunch is the main meal. But we stopped at a suco (juice) bar for a refreshing snack. Nearly every kind of fruit you can think of grows here.

For dinner we went to a churrascaria. For a set price, waiters bring you all the meat you can eat.

Tomorrow is Saturday, and our guide said restaurants will be serving feijoada, the national dish. It's a traditional meat stew served with rice and beans.

Tropical fruit in the market

A man pressing sugar

9

Minas Gerais/Ouro Preto

From Brasília we traveled more than 400 miles southeast to the city of Ouro Preto. That's in Minas Gerais state.

Ouro Preto means "black gold" in Portuguese. Brazil was a colony of Portugal for more than 300 years. Black nuggets found in the area's streams turned out to be gold mixed with iron ore.

The magnificent churches and grand public buildings we saw on our tour yesterday were a reminder that Ouro Preto was the richest mining town in Brazil for nearly 100 years.

View of Ouro Preto

Statue in Ouro Preto

Though the gold rush is over, Brazil is still a top producer of gold and gems like topaz, emeralds, and amethyst. Today we visited a mining college and the Mineralogy Museum. They have the world's largest collection of precious stones, ores, and crystals. But the most exciting part of our day was riding an antique cable car through the narrow, dark tunnels of a 250-year-old working gold mine just outside the city. Hundreds of people still work there.

Mining makes Minas Gerais one of the richest of Brazil's 26 states. Minas Gerais means "General Mines." Most of the country's deposits of iron ore and other minerals are located here. Brazil has the largest iron ore deposits in the world.

Rio de Janeiro

We've been in the seafront city of Rio de Janeiro for a few days.

Rio, as the city is often called, is the second-largest city in South America. Before the capital was moved to Brasília, Rio was Brazil's capital.

Rio is still the cultural center of Brazil. Yesterday we took the subway downtown to explore. Most of Rio's important cultural attractions—fine museums, grand theaters, and a huge library are located here.

At lunch, workers from downtown's towering office buildings and banks crowded the shops and restaurants. This reminded us that the city is still an important center of finance and industry.

Rio from the air

Bay between São Paulo and Rio de Janeiro

Rio de Janeiro from Mesa de Imperador

Cariocas—residents of Rio—don't call their city Cidade Marvilhosa (Marvelous City) because of its culture or business. It's Rio's beautiful beaches and spectacular scenery that make it one of the most-visited cities in the world.

Today we took the train to the top of the Corcovado (Hunchback Mountain) just as the sun was setting. At the peak stands one of Rio's most famous landmarks—the giant statue of Christ the Redeemer. Built to celebrate the 100th anniversary of Brazil's independence, the 130-foot statue watches over the city.

Rio de Janeiro

It always seems to be summer on the beach at Rio!

Rio's most beautiful and famous beaches are along Brazil's Atlantic coastline—the longest unbroken coastline in the world.

During the day, Cariocas and tourists like us from all over the world enjoy the warm weather and the palm-tree shaded soft, white sand. People swim, surf, and sunbathe. Others play soccer and volleyball, fly kites, jog, or exercise. Food stalls have soda, ice cream, and tasty snacks. Fruit peddlers sell ripe, golden pineapples and rough, hairy coconuts that they slice open with knives. The sweet, watery coconut milk is a treat on a hot, sunny day.

Sugarloaf Mountain in Rio de Janeiro

Volleyball players

Samba performer

On Sunday we took a break from the busy beach scene to join thousands of Cariocas at Maracana Stadium, the largest soccer stadium in the world. What we call soccer is called futebol in Brazil. It's the national sport. Every school, city, and town has a soccer field. Brazil won the World Cup championship for the fourth time in 1994.

Last night's game was very exciting! Popular players and daring plays were greeted with waving banners, pounding samba drums, and exploding firecrackers. What a night!

São Paulo

We took a short shuttle flight from Rio to São Paulo. It is Brazil's biggest city. It's also the largest city in South America. With more than 16 million people, São Paulo is also one of the fastest-growing and most-crowded cities in the world!

Paulistanos, as São Paulo's residents are called, are a colorful mixture of peoples. Most have ancestors who came here from European countries, the Middle East, or Japan. They came to work on the area's growing coffee plantations or railroads. Other Paulistanos have African or native ancestry. Because of this blend of cultures, you can find everything from bauru, a traditional Brazilian beef and cheese sandwich, to sushi at this city's great restaurants.

Fishermen mending nets

Caraguatatuba buildings

Colonial courtyard

Colonial street

São Paulo is Brazil's center of business and industry. The city produces chemicals and textiles, electrical equipment and machinery, rubber products, furniture, and processed foods. It is also Brazil's biggest car maker.

Our guide explained that Paulistanos have a reputation as the hardest workers in Brazil. But they like to enjoy themselves, too. There are lovely parks, a zoo, and lively weekend street fairs and markets. Many hard-working Paulistanos also enjoy weekend getaways to nearby beaches at Ubatuba and Caraguatatuba.

Today's tour of the Instituto Butanta was my favorite. This research center produces snakebite serum for use around the world. Thousands of poisonous snakes and other reptiles, spiders, and scorpions are studied here. We even saw a research assistant "milk" a snake's fangs for poison!

Carnival in Santa Catarina

From São Paulo we traveled 300 miles to Santa Catarina state's island capital—Florianópolis. We're here for Carnival.

Carnival is the biggest, most famous event in Brazil. It marks the days before Lent, the period leading up to Easter. Carnival is the last chance for people to party before the plain meals and serious thoughts of Lent. During Carnival, everything stops for four days of festive celebration in every town and city all over the country.

Thousands of wildly costumed people crowded the streets, eating, drinking, and dancing. In the afternoons, there were marching bands and colorful parades. You can jump right in and start dancing!

Carnival float

Woman in Carnival costume

Carnival float

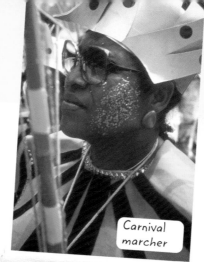

Carnival marcher

Dancer in Carnival costume

At night there were lively costume balls. We joined the fun, showering the masked dancers with confetti and streamers.

The highlight of Carnival was an exciting parade of samba schools. Samba is a popular kind of Brazilian dance and music. Samba schools are not really schools but neighborhood bands made up of hundreds of musicians and dancers. Each school chooses a theme. Samba schools spend months making the costumes, decorating the floats, and practicing the songs, skits, and dances that tell their theme's story. My favorite samba school's theme was a rain forest legend. Other schools chose themes from Brazilian history, popular television shows, and folk tales.

Carnival is the biggest, loudest, longest party I've ever been to!

19

Amazon River

Our flight today took us about 1,800 miles northwest to the city of Manaus. That's in Brazil's Amazon region. From the air, this part of the country looks like a great green carpet patterned with twisting, silvery rivers.

According to the guidebook, the Amazon region covers more than half of Brazil. This huge area is mostly made up of tropical rain forests, swamps, jungles, and 10 of the 20 largest rivers in the world. It is one of the wildest, wettest, and least-developed places on earth!

Bank of the Amazon River

Amazon sunset

Giant water lillies

The region's name comes from the Amazon River. The 4,000-mile-long Amazon is the second-longest river in the world—longer than the highway route between New York City and San Francisco! Though the Nile River in Egypt is longer, the Amazon carries more water—more than the Nile, Mississippi, and China's Yangtze rivers together!

The great Amazon begins high in the Andes Mountains of Peru and flows east across Brazil. It empties into the Atlantic Ocean.

Our guide said that the importance of Amazonia, as this area is called, is not just its water but its people, plants, animals, and natural resources. The Amazon rain forest has more kinds of plant and animal life than any other place on earth. I can't wait to start exploring!

21

Amazon River/Manaus

Our boat ride down the Amazon River begins in Manaus tomorrow.

Manaus is the capital of Brazil's largest state—Amazonas. This was once the richest city in South America. That's because cars, which had just been invented, needed rubber for tires. The rain forest surrounding Manaus had the largest supply of rubber trees in the world!

As "rubber money" poured in, Manaus's wealthy settlers built a grand city. Ships brought the finest building materials from all over Europe. There were parks, fountains, museums, mansions, theaters, electric lights, and streetcars—all surrounded by the largest, densest forests on earth!

Joining of the Black River and the Amazon River

House on bank of the Amazon

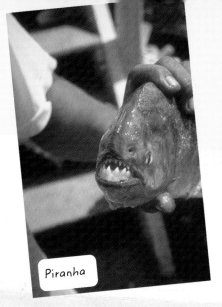
Piranha

Fish market

Though the rubber boom is long over, Manaus remains an important inland port. Ships bring in clothing, food, tools, and other products. They pick up tropical fruits and vegetables, nuts, fresh fish, lumber, and rubber.

Today we visited the city's museums dedicated to the history and culture of the region's native peoples. Our guide explained that Brazil's native peoples are slowly disappearing. Over the years, disease, slavery, and the destruction of the rain forest have taken their toll. From an estimated 900 different tribes that lived here when the Portuguese arrived, approximately 200 are left. Most live in protected areas the government has set aside for them. Some still live by hunting, fishing, gathering, and simple farming. Others live in permanent villages and have adopted modern ways.

23

Wildlife

It's taking our boat a week to travel east down the Amazon River to the port city of Belém. There's so much to see. Our guide said many of the plants and animals we might see cannot be found anywhere else on earth!

There are more than 1,600 species of birds alone. About 30 different kinds of monkeys also live in the trees. So does the giant three-toed sloth who eats, sleeps, and has its babies hanging upside down!

Tapir

Luna moth

Capybara

Parrot

Large beetle

On the ground there are tapirs and anteaters. Capybaras—the world's largest rodents—also live here. Jaguars, panthers, and snakes slink among the trees. More than 200 species of snakes live in the rain forest. The anaconda, the world's largest snake, can grow as long as 40 feet (I hope we don't see one of those)!

About 3,000 species of fish live in the Amazon. There are sharks and pink freshwater dolphins, electric eels, meat-eating piranhas, and huge pirarucu, the world's largest freshwater fish. As we found out later, many of the river's fish make tasty meals.

Jewel-colored butterflies darted among the flowers. More than 4,000 kinds of butterflies live in the rain forest—some are bigger than birds. Scientists also think as many as 30 million different kinds of insect species may live here—including spiders large enough to eat birds!

25

Flora

It's raining again! The rain forest gets an average yearly rainfall of 50-120 inches.

Plants grow best where it's warm and wet. There's no shortage of either here! The hot, humid rain forest has tens of thousands of plant species. About 3,000 species of trees have been found in just one square mile. Most are giants, soaring between 80 and 100 feet tall. The Brazil nut tree can grow as tall as a ten-story building!

Plants in the rain forest grow in layers. The top layer, or canopy, is made up of the tallest tree tops. Below the canopy is the gloomy understory. This is where thick vines twist around tree trunks or dangle from the branches above. The forest floor is littered with leaves and branches. The leaves block so much sun that we needed flashlights to get around—even at noon!

Yellow swallowtail

Wild orchid

Bird of paradise flower

Sadly, the amazing rain forest is shrinking. Loggers, miners, ranchers, and farmers destroy thousands of trees each day. The greatest damage is caused by slashing-and-burning. That's when trees are cut down and the cleared area is burned to destroy the stumps and other plants.

Our guide explained that the Amazon rain forest protects the entire planet. Nick-named the earth's "lungs," it replenishes nearly one-half of the world's supply of oxygen. It also helps prevent "global warming" caused by the greenhouse effect—when the sun's heat is trapped in the atmosphere by layers of pollution.

Belém

We finally arrived in Belém this morning. We're on the Para River—a river that branches off from the Amazon.

Ships of all kinds and sizes dock here. Along the waterfront was the Ver-O-Peso market.

The market's most interesting section was filled with rain forest plants—herbs, roots, leaves, and bark. Rain forest plants are used in perfumes, insecticides, foods, fuels, and oils. Most importantly, our guide said that the rain forest is like a giant natural drugstore. About one-fourth of all the world's medicines come from the rain forest. Some scientists believe that cures for cancer, AIDS, and other diseases may someday be discovered among these plants!

Selling herbs, plants, and roots

Olinda/Recife

Last night, we flew about 1,000 miles southeast to Recife. This is a coastal city of canals and bridges, beaches, modern skyscrapers, museums, and crafts workshops.

Beautiful nearby Olinda is filled with amazing colonial architecture. Its narrow streets were lined with brightly painted homes and fancy decorated churches.

Recife and Olinda were important centers of the colonial sugar trade. They were ruled by the Portuguese for many years. Then the area was invaded by the Dutch in the 1600s. The Dutch ruled for more than 20 years before the Portuguese regained control.

Olinda

Church, Olinda

Arts & Crafts

The market, Mercado Modelo, was packed with stalls offering arts and crafts from Brazil's mix of European, African, and Indian cultures. There were ceramic figures, wood carvings, and delicate lacework. There were also sturdy woven hammocks, jewelry of feathers and animal teeth, and jewelry of gold and gems. Among a stall filled with baskets, leather goods, and musical instruments, a man was blowing huge vases out of glass.

Master glassblower

Folk-art shop

Salvador

In Salvador we got to visit two cities in one! Salvador was the first Portuguese capital of Brazil before Rio and Brasília. It was divided into an upper and lower city during colonial times.

At sea level, the lower city contains a 400-year-old fort, docks, and the commercial district. A towering 200-foot-high elevator shaft connects the cities and is Salvador's largest landmark. The historic upper city contains grand public buildings, elegant mansions, and fancy colonial churches.

African influences are everywhere. Street vendors sell fragrant palm oil, peanuts, and coconut milk. One evening we visited a terreiro, or Candomble church. Candomble is a religion that mixes African folk beliefs with Catholic symbols. We also saw a demonstration of Capoeira, a dance-like kind of martial arts first developed by slaves to disguise fighting.

Capoeira in action

Glossary

Ancestry members of a person's family that lived in the past.

Colony a territory that has been settled by people from another country and is controlled by that country.

Equator an imaginary line around the center of Earth, halfway between the North and South poles.

Plantation a large farm found in warm climates that grows crops such as coffee and cotton.

Serum a liquid used to prevent or cure a disease.

Slum an overcrowded, poor, and neglected area of housing in a town or city.

Species one of the groups into which plants or animals with the same characteristics are divided.

Textile a cloth or fabric that has been woven or knitted.

For More Information

Books

Dahl, Michael S. *Brazil*. Minneapolis, MN: Capstone, 1997.

Dawson, Zoe. *Brazil* (Postcards). Chatham, NJ: Raintree/Steck Vaughn, 1995.

Enderlein, Cheryl L. *Celebrating Birthdays in Brazil* (Birthdays Around the World). Danbury, CT: Grolier Publications, 1998.

Waterlow, Julia. *A Family From Brazil* (Families Around the World). Chatham, NJ: Raintree/Steck Vaughn, 1998.

Web Site
Rain Forests

Questions and answers about the Brazilian rain forests—www.wideopen.igc.apc.org/ran/kids_action/questions.

Index